michael morpurgo

Cover illustrations by Cecilia Johannson
Interior illustrations by Shoo Rayner

Mudpuddle
Farm

HarperCollins *Children's Books*

happy meal

First published in Great Britain in hardback
by A&C Black (Publishers) Limited in 1995
First published in paperback by Collins,
a division of HarperCollins*Publishers* Ltd in 1996

This edition published by HarperCollins *Children's Books* in 2012
HarperCollins *Children's Books* is a division of HarperCollins*Publishers* Ltd,
77-85 Fulham Palace Road, Hammersmith, London, W6 8JB.

The HarperCollins website address is: www.harpercollins.co.uk

1

Text copyright © Michael Morpurgo 1995
Illustrations copyright © Shoo Rayner 1995
Made for McDonald's 2012. The Golden Arches and Happy Meal Logos are
registered trademarks of and © McDonald's Corporation and its affiliates.

ISBN 978-0-00-790344-3

The author and illustrator assert the moral right to be
identified as the author and illustrator of the work.

Printed and bound in England by Clays Ltd, St Ives plc

Chapter One

There was once a family of all sorts of animals that lived in the farmyard behind the tumbledown barn on Mudpuddle Farm.

At first light every morning Frederick, the flame-feathered cockerel, lifted his eyes to the sun and crowed and crowed until the light came on in old Farmer Rafferty's bedroom window.

One . . . . by . . . . one,
the animals crept out into the dawn . . .

. . . and stretched . . .

4

. . . and yawned . . .

. . . and scratched themselves.

But no one ever spoke a word, not
until after breakfast.

One morning, Captain was crunching away at his last mouthful of breakfast hay when he noticed something was wrong.

Someone was missing.

Albertine and her little goslings were preening themselves on their island.

Upside and Down were upside down in the pond.

Peggoty and her little piglets, including Pintsize, snuffled and snorted around the dung heap.

Diana the silly sheep, who couldn't count to save her life, was counting the clouds.

Penelope and her chicks scratched and scuffled in the orchard, never too far from Frederick.

Grace and Primrose grazed nose to nose in the meadow.

Jigger, the almost-always-sensible sheepdog, was chasing his tail again.

And Mossop, the cat with the one and single eye, was curled up asleep on his tractor seat as he always was.

BUT, where was Egbert the grumbly goat?

Jigger, have you seen that grumbly goat?

Nope, I'll have a look, shall I?

So Jigger looked and looked.

...paper sacks in the shed...

...nor was he chewing

NIP

Hmmm!

WOOSH!

Egbert wasn't anywhere. He'd done
a bunk, buzzed off, gone walkabout.

11

If anyone knows where he is,
thought Jigger, Albertine does,
because Albertine always knows
everything. So Jigger ran down to
the pond.

Albertine, have you seen
Egbert anywhere? He seems
to have gone missing.

But Egbert did not come back. The animals searched here, there and everywhere for him.

But it was no good, he couldn't find him anywhere. No one could find him.

'I can't think where he's gone,' said
Auntie Grace, the dreamy-eyed cow.
'Nor me,' said Primrose, who
always agreed with her.

I don't know
where he's gone
either.

'I know, I know,'
said Diana, the
silly sheep.

He's gone
missing!

'Don't worry,' Albertine told her
little goslings.

That goat will be
back, you'll see, around
suppertime, I should think

she's so
reassuring.

Chapter Two

Sure enough, just as old Farmer Rafferty was giving all the animals their supper that evening, Egbert wandered into the yard, grumbling as usual.

'Egbert, where have you been?' asked
Farmer Rafferty in the nasty, raspy
voice he kept for special occasions.

I've been looking for
you everywhere!

'Worried sick we were,' said
Captain, the carthorse whom
everyone loved and who loved
everyone.

But Egbert wouldn't say another
word about it.

Down on her island in the pond, Albertine shook her head, smiled her goosey smile and thought deep goosey thoughts.

I told you he'd come back, didn't I? I'll tell you something else too, just so long as you keep mum, if you know what I mean. That goat's been up to something.

what? What? What?

Who knows? who knows? Now, let's watch the sun go down, and then we'll all go to sleep.

Chapter Three

It wasn't long after this that Egbert
began behaving very strangely
indeed. For one thing, he stopped
grumbling. Everyone thought he
must be sick, but he wasn't.

Are you
feeling alright,
Egbert?

Enigmatic Smile

'Good morning,' he'd say as he passed by,

...and isn't it a fine one too?

Isn't it a good day to be alive?

And he'd say that with the wind whistling through the farmyard and the rain thundering down on the corrugated roofs.

Then one day, Diana the silly sheep
saw something very, very strange.
She saw Egbert dancing! And he
was singing too!

la la la la la la

Of course none of the animals believed her at first, because Diana was always silly. But she told them and told them until they had to come and look.

I'm singing in the rain...... I'm singing

See?

And of course, when they saw it with their own eyes they had to believe it. Egbert was dancing in the puddles, and singing his heart out.

in the rain... what a wonderful feeling I'm happy again

SPLISH

SPLOOSH

SPLASH

SPLOSH

'He's really sick,'
said Jigger sadly.

'Hope it's not catching,' said
Penelope, hurrying her chicks away.

'He's gone loopy, if you ask me,' said
Peggoty, keeping her distance at the
top of the dung heap.

Mossop opened his one and single
eye and shut it again.

I'm having a bad
dream about a singing,
dancing goat that's lost
his marbles. I think
he ought to see a vet.

But Auntie Grace and Primrose liked
the song so much that they found a
puddle of their own and joined in.

♪ Gimme the Moo-nlight...
Gimme the Moo-sic ♪

Albertine sighed and smiled
secretly to herself.

What's up with that goat?

Sigh!

'You'd never understand, Captain,' said Albertine; and Captain felt very stupid.

Captain couldn't understand what Albertine was talking about, but he didn't want to say so, in case she might think he was as stupid as he felt he was.

Chapter Four

It was Tuesday, and Tuesday was always the day old Farmer Rafferty went off to market.

My day out.

He put on his best jacket and his best hat. Then he scooped Mossop off his tractor seat and drove to market.

I'm singing in the hum-te-hum ti tun

Off he went, happy as a lark,
singing to himself as he always did
when he was happy, though he could
never remember the words.

But old Farmer Rafferty had
forgotten something else too.
Something much more important
than the words. He had forgotten to
close his vegetable garden gate.

Later that morning, Egbert was
feeling even hungrier than usual.

I've chewed the last of the paint
off the gate. I've eaten the last
of the paper sacks. I've nearly eaten
my rope, but I'm still hungry.

CREAK
RUMBLE
GROAN

Then he saw Farmer Rafferty's
garden gate swinging in the wind,
squeaking on its hinges.

'Carrots,' he thought. 'Apples.'

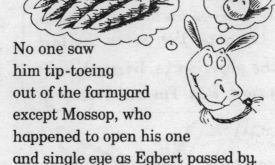

No one saw
him tip-toeing
out of the farmyard
except Mossop, who
happened to open his one
and single eye as Egbert passed by.

My goat dream again, only now he's on his tip-toes and ballet dancing!

And he went back to sleep to finish
his dream.

All morning long, Egbert chomped and chewed his way through old Farmer Rafferty's carrots. No one noticed what he was up to until after lunch.

Early in the afternoon, Peggoty was taking her piglets for a stroll. As usual, Pintsize had run on ahead. That was why he reached the garden gate first. Pintsize knew, and all the animals knew, that none of them (except Mossop because he was special), was ever allowed inside old Farmer Rafferty's vegetable garden.

Afternoon, Mossop.

So when he saw Egbert standing in the middle of the vegetable garden with a carrot in his mouth, he knew that there was going to be trouble, big trouble.

Eeek!

Pintsize loved it when other people got into trouble for a change.

Peggoty could not believe her eyes.
There wasn't a single carrot left
except the one in Egbert's mouth.

Is something
the matter,
Peggoty?

The little piglets gasped. Peggoty let
out her screechiest scream and
called for help.

Captain! Jigger! Albertine! Come quick, come quick!

And all the animals came running as fast as they could.

What's the matter?

'Egbert!' cried Captain. 'Out of there! Out of there! If old Farmer Rafferty catches you in his vegetable garden your goose will be cooked!' And then he thought about what he'd said.

Oh, I'm sorry, Albertine.

munch

munch

But Albertine just smiled.

See? I told you Captain, didn't I? Carrots.

But Captain still didn't understand.

'I'll get him out,' said Jigger, the almost-always-sensible sheepdog. He dashed into the garden and tried to pull Egbert out by his rope. But Egbert would not budge.

Captain came in to help as well, but still Egbert dug his heels in and would not move.

Oh, come on, Egbert. Old Farmer Rafferty will be back in a minute.

In fact, old Farmer Rafferty was just at the end of the farm lane, talking to Farmer Farley from the next-door farm. 'Goats,' Farmer Farley was saying, 'who'd have them? They go where they want, eat what they want, do as they please. Still, they make you laugh, don't they?' And the two of them just laughed and laughed.

Back in the farmyard, the animals all heard Farmer Rafferty coming up the lane on his tractor. He was still singing away.

'I'm off,' said Jigger.

'Me too,' said Captain.

But Albertine decided to wait.
'I think I'll just stay and see what
happens,' she said.

Pintsize hid under Albertine's wings
and pretended to be a gosling.

As old Farmer Rafferty came through the garden gate, all the animals hid behind the wall and watched.

Suddenly, old Farmer Rafferty stopped singing. With bated breath, the animals waited for him to shout in his nasty, raspy voice. But he didn't.

All he said was:

You silly old goat, eating all my lovely carrots. Still, I expect you need them more than I do.

And Farmer Rafferty laughed and laughed. He picked up Egbert's rope and led him out into the orchard.

You have all the apples you can find, my dear. You'll get fat, but that doesn't matter, does it? You eat as much as you like.

The animals could not believe their ears. They could not understand it at all. But Albertine could. She smiled her goosey smile and waddled off back to her pond. Then she climbed up on to her island and tucked her head under her wing and slept. There were four little goslings under her wing that night, and one of them had trotters.

Chapter Five

It turned out just as old Farmer
Rafferty had said. Egbert did get
fat, very fat. It wasn't surprising –
he did nothing but eat all day long.

He ate anything and everything –

Captain's
best hay,

Jigger's
biscuits,

Peggoty's
pigmeal,

Penelope's
corn,

Diana's
sheepnuts,

and old Farmer Rafferty's socks off the washing line.

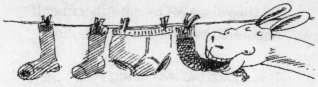

He even ate the sack that Mossop used for his bed on the tractor seat. 'I'm not dreaming this,' said Mossop, yawning hugely. 'That goat is eating my bed.' Mossop was not at all happy about that.

Right, that's the last straw. What are we going to do about that goat?

No one knew what to do, but they all knew something had to be done. So they went off to ask Albertine. If anyone knew what to do, she did.

But Albertine was being very secretive. 'Mum's the word,' she said inscrutably, and she would say no more.

'Well, I think that goat needs to lose some weight,' said Auntie Grace, the dreamy-eyed cow.

'Jogging,' said Jigger.

So five times a day all the animals, except Albertine, who thought it was all very silly, jogged round Front Meadow. Afterwards they did their aerobics, and all the while Egbert would sing along quite happily, and dance in any puddles he could find.

Ridiculous!

'I'm singing in the sun, singing in the sun,' (or rain, depending on the weather). He didn't seem to mind the exercise at all, just so long as he could carry on eating afterwards.

And that's just what he did. He got fatter,

and fatter,

and fatter.

And to everyone's amazement, he stopped grumbling completely. The animals could not believe it.

'I'm just the happiest, luckiest goat in the whole wide world,' he said, jumping into another puddle.

'What's he got to be so happy about?' said Jigger. 'What's happened to him?' And he went to ask Albertine again.

But Albertine was keeping mum.
'Mum's the word,' she said
inscrutably, and she smiled a secret
goosey smile again.

Chapter Six

Then one morning, Captain was looking out of his stable after his breakfast, when he saw that Egbert had vanished again.

No one could find him anywhere. All day long they looked but they still couldn't find him.

At last they went to tell old Farmer
Rafferty the bad news.

We've lost him again, we've lost Egbert!

But instead of saddling Captain and
going out to look for him, old
Farmer Rafferty just leant on his
spade and laughed and laughed.

Why don't
you have a
look through
my sitting
room window?

POW   ZIP

Jigger got there first.

'Oh, yes he can,' laughed old
Farmer Rafferty. 'He can and he
has because *he* is a *she*.
Egbert is Egberta,
and she's just had
two lovely kids.'

And they all peered in at the window. There was Egberta lying out on the sofa, a cushion under her head, with her two little kids beside her.

That evening, Farmer Farley
brought Billy, his billygoat, over to
Farmer Rafferty's to see his kids.

'It's my Egberta who's the clever one, bless her,' said Farmer Rafferty.

'I'd say they're both clever,' said Farmer Farley.

Meanwhile, Billy chewed the paint off the window and Egberta chewed the sofa, and both of them looked very happy indeed.

Chapter Seven

Out on the pond, Upside and Down came up for a breather. 'Anything new happened?' they asked.

Egbert's not fat any more.

You're kidding!

'Not me,' Albertine smiled. 'Egberta. She's the one that's kidding. It'll be nice to have some real kids around, won't it, children?'

She cuddled her goslings under her wings, including the one with the trotters. 'Do you want a story to send you to sleep?' And of course they did.

The night came down, the moon came up and everyone slept on Mudpuddle Farm.